balloon

 finish line

 basket

 go

 bird

 prize

 butterfly

 rainbow

 camera

 sun

 cheese

 tree

 cloud

 wind

The Big
Balloon Race

by Jennifer Frantz

illustrated by

the Thompson Bros. and Eric Binder

HarperFestival®
A Division of HarperCollins*Publishers*

It was a perfect day

in Pony Park.

The ☀ was shining.

The 🐦🐦 were singing.

The 〰 was blowing

just right.

A fluffy white ☁

floated in the sky.

"What a sweet day for the race!" said Fluttershy.

"Say !" she said, holding up her .

"," said Minty.

"This is going to be

the best race ever!"

said Butterscotch.

Easy for her to say,

thought Daisy Jo.

She always wins the .

Daisy Jo wanted to win

the this year.

"Racers ready?"

"All set!" called Fluttershy

from her .

"This is ready to !"

said Butterscotch.

"Which way is the ?"

asked Minty.

"On your marks, get set, !"

The took off into the sky.

"*Whee!* I feel like a !" said Daisy Jo.

"I feel like a !" called Minty.

Daisy Jo's
was in the lead.

Butterscotch was

right behind her.

Minty was off

chasing a .

A big gust of ⧫ blew.

Butterscotch's

shot ahead.

But she was headed

for a 🌳 !

Butterscotch's got

caught on a .

Daisy Jo could see

the , but she had

to help her friend.

"Climb into my ,"

she said.

The blew Daisy Jo and Butterscotch across the FINISH.

They won the race together!

A huge filled the sky over Pony Park.

"Smile for the 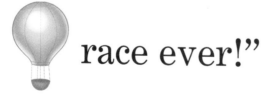 !" said Fluttershy.

" 🧀 !" said Daisy Jo and Butterscotch while holding up their 🏆.

"This *was* the best 🎈 race ever!" said Butterscotch.

"Winning is fun,"

said Daisy Jo.

"But a good friend is

the best  of all!"